**Dad**

**Mum**

**Lu**

**m**

**Lucy**

**Will**

**Dad**

**Mum**

**Lu**

**n**

**Lucy**

**Will**

# The Quigleys
at Large

# The Quigleys
# at Large

## Simon Mason
### *Illustrated by Helen Stephens*

**David Fickling Books**

OXFORD · NEW YORK

A DAVID FICKLING BOOK

Published by David Fickling Books
an imprint of Random House Children's Books
a division of Random House, Inc.
New York

Copyright © 2003 by Simon Mason

Illustrations copyright © 2003 by Helen Stephens

Published simultaneously in Canada by Random House of Canada Limited, Toronto.
Originally published in Great Britain by David Fickling Books,
an imprint of Random House Children's Books

www.randomhouse.com/kids

*Library of Congress Cataloging-in-Publication Data*
Mason, Simon, 1962–
The Quigleys at large / Simon Mason ; illustrated by Helen Stephens.— 1st American ed.
p. cm.
Summary: The further adventures and misadventures of the four members of the Quigley family—
Mum, Dad, Lucy, and Will.
ISBN 0-385-75022-6 (trade)—ISBN 0-385-75031-5 (lib. bdg.)
[1. Family life—England—Fiction. 2. Humorous stories. 3. England—Fiction.]
I. Stephens, Helen, 1972– ill. II. Title.
PZ7.M4232Qv 2003
[Fic]—dc21
2003047036

Printed in the United States of America
October 2003

10 9 8 7 6 5 4 3 2 1
First American Edition

*To Gwilym and Eleri*

# Contents

# Dad in Trouble

# Dad in Trouble

It was Saturday morning, and the Quigleys were sitting in the back room eating breakfast in their pyjamas and dressing gowns. In a cage on top of the toy cupboard there were two budgies, one green and one blue, and they were eating their breakfast too. They went *tuckle, tuckle, natter, natter, natter.*

This wasn't the only noise. There was a thudding.

Without looking up from the newspaper, Dad asked Will to stop bouncing his tennis ball against the wall just above his head. Will put the ball down next to his bowl of porridge, and looked at it. He gave it a little push, and it rolled slowly across the table. The Quigleys' table was a very good table for rolling things across. The ball slid between the pint of milk and the jug of orange juice, nudged its way round Dad's bowl of cornflakes, and eventually dropped onto the newspaper in Dad's lap.

Dad looked up and opened his mouth.

'Did you know this table slopes?' Will asked. 'I was just testing it, just now, and I've discovered it slopes.'

Mum said, 'It's been sloping since the year before Lucy was born. Anyway, someone's coming to fix it next week.'

Dad went back to reading the paper.

Will looked round the room. 'There's something wrong with those curtains as well,' he said after a while.

'Yes,' Mum said. 'Ever since you showed us that climbing move. We've ordered new ones.'

Will thought a bit more. 'I suppose you know the fridge door doesn't shut properly,' he said. 'And the window in our room won't open.'

'Enough,' Dad said irritably. Dad had worked late every night for a week, and he was very tired. When he was in that mood almost any topic of conversation, even sensible and interesting ones like sloping tables and busted fridge doors, made him mad.

There was a knock at the door, and Lucy ran to answer it. She held part of her breakfast in one hand, and stood on the

skirting board and turned the latch with the other, and pulled the door open a few inches. She could do this, just. A man stood on the doorstep.

'What have you come to fix?' she asked. 'Is it the fridge door? Or our window?'

'The piano,' the man said.

'I don't think there's anything wrong with the piano,' she said. 'Will?'

'I've come to tune it,' the man said.

After a while, Lucy let him in. Mum took him into the front room, and he got out his instruments and lifted up the top of the piano and started to poke around inside. Mum and Lucy watched. Lucy was still holding her breakfast, which she had forgotten about.

Will drifted in. He was feeling bored and restless.

He said, 'Does anyone want to hear my new laugh? I've been practising a new laugh. It's a good one. It's a fake laugh.'

'Go back into the kitchen,' Mum said. 'We're busy.'

In the kitchen, Dad was still eating breakfast. Or rather not eating, just sitting, staring at the newspaper, his eyes half-closed. Will wondered if he'd fallen asleep sitting down. He'd read that some people can train themselves to fall asleep anywhere, in any position, and he wondered if Dad had trained himself.

There was a sudden high-pitched scream in Dad's left ear, and he rose a couple of inches off his chair, scattering the pages of the paper onto the floor as he fell.

'Do you like my new laugh?' Will said. 'It's my fake laugh. Do you want to hear it again?'

Dad was cross, but Will was restless and bored and wouldn't listen.

'It's just a laugh, Dad. Everyone laughs. Lucy does. Lucy, do a fake laugh.'

Lucy, who had come in from the living room, made a noise like a nearly dead animal.

Will said, 'That's really good, Lucy. Now it's your turn, Dad. What's your fake laugh like?'

Dad was still picking up the newspaper from the floor. 'I haven't got a fake laugh,' he said crossly.

'You have, I've heard it.'

'Enough,' Dad said. 'Enough of all this pestering.' He looked around, as if for help, and his eyes fell on the budgies. 'The budgies need cleaning out,' he said to Will, with some satisfaction. 'I'll get them down, and you can clean them.'

Will protested. 'But I never clean them,' he said. 'It's not my job. It's your job.'

This was true. Somehow it had become Dad's job to look after Will's budgies. He didn't know how this had happened. Somehow Will was always too busy, or it was too late, or else he was doing his homework instead.

'But they're your budgies,' Dad said.

'But it's your job,' Will said.

Dad opened his mouth to say something else, but at that moment Mum called Will from the front room, and without waiting to hear what else Dad had to say, Will turned and left.

Dad lifted down the cage. The two budgies hopped from perch to perch as it swayed. The blue one was called Roaring Wind, and the green one was called Deathwing, Lord of the Skies. Will had been doing the Aztecs at school when he gave them their names. Roaring Wind was calm and quiet. Deathwing, Lord of the Skies was mad and loud.

First Dad made sure the French windows were closed, then he lifted up the top of the cage. Roaring Wind hopped out calmly and flew up to the curtain rail, where he always perched. Deathwing, Lord of the Skies flew round and round in small, fierce circles, squawking loudly, and Dad had to shake the cage to get him to fly out.

'That bird has the brains of a dishcloth,' Dad said. The birds eyed him from the curtain rail like two old men on a park bench. 'Fly?' they seemed to say. 'What do you think we are? Birds?' Of course they didn't actually say anything. The man in

the shop had said they could learn to talk, but they hadn't. They squatted on the curtain rail in silence.

Dad removed the soiled gritpaper from the bottom of the cage. He cleaned the empty cage with a brush and washed it in the sink. He scrubbed the budgies' toy ladder and mirror, replaced the old perch covers with fresh ones, filled the drinking container with clean water and fastened a new piece of cuttlefish bone to the cage's bars. Roaring Wind and Deathwing, Lord of the Skies sat very still on the curtain rail, watching him work.

'Fly, why don't you?' Dad said. Will's book said they were meant to fly for ten minutes every day. Dad jumped up and down, waving his arms at them, but it made no difference. They huddled closer together. Leaving them on the curtain rail, he took the seed hoppers outside to blow away the old husks.

As he stood over the dustbins the piano tuner went past.

'All done,' the man said.

'Don't suppose you know anything about how to make budgies fly, do you?' Dad asked.

'Why? Something wrong with their wings?'

'It's not their wings that are a problem,' Dad said. 'It's their brains.'

He went to see if he could find Will's budgie book on the shelves in the front room, but he couldn't. He couldn't find it

because the room was a mess. The
Quigleys' front room was often a mess. For
a minute or two, Dad half-heartedly tidied
it. He cleared away half a dozen of the
worst unwashed beakers which had been left
along the bookshelves.
He gathered armfuls of
*The Beano* from all
corners of the room and
wedged them tightly
into the space between
the bookcase and the
piano in such a way
that if one were pulled
out they would all
immediately fall onto
the rug. He put down
the piano lid which the
tuner had left up and
nearly flattened the end
of his finger. And he
wiped the remains of
Lucy's breakfast off the
sole of his right shoe.

But he still couldn't find Will's budgie book, so he went into the back room again.

He poured fresh seed into the hoppers. He chopped up some apple and banana, and put the pieces on a saucer at the bottom of the cage.

'Now for you two birdbrains,' he said. He looked up at the top of the curtains. Roaring Wind was sitting on the rail looking back at him. But there was no sign of Deathwing, Lord of the Skies.

Dad glanced round the room. 'You don't mean to tell me he's been *flying*?' he said to Roaring Wind. Roaring Wind was giving nothing away.

Irritated, Dad began to search round the room. He jumped up to check the tops of the kitchen cabinets, and knelt down to look under the toy cupboard, but he couldn't see Deathwing anywhere. He was just getting annoyed when he saw that the window above the sink was wide open. For a moment he stood looking at it, completely still.

'Oh no,' he said at last. He stood there for a moment longer, then ran out of the room.

For the rest of the morning, the Quigleys walked round the back garden looking up into the trees. All the back gardens in the street were the same, long and narrow, overflowing with trees and flowers and bushes. Will used his binoculars. Deathwing,

Lord of the Skies was nowhere to be seen.

'Why couldn't you have just closed the window?' he asked Dad for the eighth time.

Dad looked sorry for the eighth time. 'I forgot,' he said. 'I didn't expect him to actually fly.'

'You're in big trouble,' Will said.

'I think we'll find him,' Lucy said. She didn't have binoculars but she did have the inside of a toilet roll.

'Yes, I think he'll come back,' Mum said. 'He'll miss Roaring Wind.' They'd put the cage with Roaring Wind in it on the garden table, for encouragement.

'I bet he's in Singapore by now,' Dad said in a low voice to Mum.

After a while Will began to cry, and Mum, Dad and Lucy comforted him.

'Think of it this way,' Dad said. He used his gentle voice. 'Even if he doesn't come back, he's free. He'll have a lovely life nesting in the trees, and flying round in the fresh air getting up to all sorts of tricks and jokes.'

'Shut up,' Will said. Will was very angry with Dad.

'Now, Will,' Mum said.

'It's not your budgie that's gone into the wild to die. This isn't his habitat. These are the wrong sorts of trees, and the wrong sort of fresh air.'

While Mum made lunch, Will sat on the lawn by himself. He remembered the things Deathwing, Lord of the Skies used to do, the way he cocked his head on one side, the way his eyes went big when you pushed your finger towards him, the way he shot from side to side of the cage when he was excited. Will put his face in his arms and sat on the grass feeling sad. He was so sad he didn't hear the noise at first. And when he did hear it, he thought he was imagining it and sat without moving, his face still in his arms, while the noise that seemed to be in his head went *tuckle, tuckle, natter, natter, natter.* He hardly believed it even when he lifted his head and looked up into the chestnut tree at the corner of the garden,

and saw, high up on a branch, a familiar
green bird looking down at him.

'*Tuckle, tuckle,*' the bird said. And then it
flew away out of sight.

Will ran into the house.

After that, the Quigleys spotted him several
times. He seemed to be staying close to the
house. Mum saw him in the ash tree, and
Will saw him again flitting between the
summer house and the holly bush.

'I saw him too,' Lucy said.

'Where?' Will said.

She couldn't remember. She pointed to the end of her toilet roll.

Over lunch the Quigleys held a meeting to plan how to recapture him.

'What about tranquilliser darts?' Will said.

'He's not a rhino, Will,' Mum said.

'Well, what's your idea?' Will said.

Mum said, 'What about dusters?'

'Dusters?'

'I remember reading that it confuses a budgie if you throw a duster over it.'

Dad said that if they could find someone who could throw a duster accurately fifty feet upwards into a chestnut tree and get it to land on top of a bird measuring no more than twenty centimetres from beak to tail, he was very much in favour of it.

They sat in silence for a while.

Lucy said she thought that birdsong might work, and that if they didn't know any birdsong, perhaps some other sort of song would do. She remembered that she

could play 'Sing, Bird, Sing' on the
recorder. Everyone agreed that, whatever
plan they came up with, she should play
'Sing, Bird, Sing' while they tried it.

'What about just calling him?' Mum said.

'He's too stupid,' Dad said.

Will said this wasn't true. Will asked who'd left the window open.

'All right, all right,' Dad said. 'But it's not as if he's going to answer you. The bird's a mute. I think food is our best bet. We'll put out some food to attract his attention.'

Later in the afternoon they filled a stack of plastic dishes with five different types of seed, two dozen sprigs of millet, thirty-four budgie treats on sticks and a wide selection of exotic fruit, and positioned them round the garden – on the summer house roof, in the lower branches of the chestnut and ash trees, on the patio, on both fences and

across the lawn. Then they went into the house, and hid.

After a while some starlings flew down and began to feast.

Dad ran out and chased them
away, and hid again.

Some time later, Lucy
suggested she play 'Sing, Bird,
Sing'.

She played it seventeen times
on the trot.

Just when they thought it
wasn't going to work, Will
said, 'Look!' There was a
green flash from behind the summer house,
and the budgie landed on the edge of the
patio, near one of the dishes of food.

'What do we do now, Dad?' Will
whispered.

Dad hesitated. Mum handed him a
duster. After giving her a look, he put the
duster in his mouth and crawled very
quietly out of the French windows. He
looked a bit like a dog, or perhaps a sloth.
He went very slowly, and when he was
halfway across the patio the budgie flew
away. Dad took the duster out of his mouth
and spat twice. 'Next time,' he said, 'at least

can I have a clean duster?'

All the Quigleys now armed themselves with dusters and hid themselves round the garden. Almost as soon as they were in position, the budgie flew down again, and began to eat the millet suspended from the summer house roof. This time Lucy was the nearest. She tiptoed out from behind the wheelbarrow, and began to walk, very, very slowly, towards the summer house. She was so excited she could hardly walk straight, and she nearly fell into the flowerbed. Out of the corner of her eye she could see Will making furious gestures with his duster, but she ignored him. When she was about three feet away from him, the budgie stopped feeding and hopped to one side, and looked at her nervously. To put him at his ease she began to hum 'Sing, Bird, Sing' as softly and prettily as she could. Deathwing, Lord of the Skies flew away. Out of the corner of her eye, she saw Will fall to the ground and beat the grass with his hands.

For two or three hours the Quigleys hid and crept and pounced and threw their dusters, and Deathwing, Lord of the Skies flew in and out of the trees in a playful sort of way.

'Right,' Dad said at last. 'It's time to get serious.' He went to get the car keys. 'I'm not fooling around any more.'

When he came back from town half an hour later, he had with him a ten-metre roll of fine gardener's netting, a fat coil of green twine, a hoolah hoop and a toasting fork.

For a while he hid in the front room and

wouldn't let anyone in. He'd taken the tool box in with him. There were sounds of sawing and hammering. Eventually he came out, and, without speaking to anyone, went into the garden carrying what looked like an enormous, partly-destroyed fishing net. He looked very determined. It wasn't his natural look, and it made him look a bit cross-eyed.

'What's that big ripped knickers thing, Dad?' Lucy asked.

Dad didn't say anything. In fact they didn't know if he could talk while he was looking determined, his mouth was so tight shut.

On the lawn he set up his invention. Part of the hoolah hoop had been sawn away to make it horseshoe-shaped, and the end of the net had been stapled round the rim of what remained. Dad stood the hoolah hoop on its sawn-off ends, and propped it up with the toasting fork. Then he spread the netting out behind to form a sort of tunnel. In the mouth of the tunnel he placed a trail of seed and millet, and inside he made an enormous mound of all the exotic fruit, which he gathered from all the dishes round the garden. Then, gently tying one end of the twine to the toasting fork, he retreated carefully towards a nearby buddleia, paying out the twine behind him. Putting his finger to his lips, he disappeared behind the bush.

'What's wrong with Dad, Mum?' Lucy

asked. 'Why is he in the bush?'

'It's a trap,' Will said excitedly. 'It's a great, big, mad trap for budgies. It'll never work,' he added sadly.

'Will it work, Mum?' Lucy asked. 'Is Dad good at traps?'

Mum looked unsure. 'Well, once he built a barbecue,' she said. 'That turned out to be a bit of a trap.'

They went into the house, and watched from the back room. For half an hour nothing happened. Occasionally Dad shifted position behind the bush with a slight groan.

'What if Deathwing, Lord of the Skies was watching all the time?' Lucy whispered.

'Perhaps he wouldn't have understood what Dad was doing,' Mum whispered back. 'Dad thinks he isn't very clever.'

'I'd like to know what he thinks of Dad,' Will whispered.

Then there was a movement on the lawn, and they silently pressed to the French windows. A green budgie stood on the

grass, its head cocked on one side. For a
while it looked around, then hopped
towards the trail of millet and seed, and
looked round again.

It wasn't quite under the netting.

Will crossed his fingers.

After a minute it took another step
towards the large pile of fruit, and stopped,
and looked round again. It seemed to be
looking at Dad's bush.

It still wasn't quite under the netting. Will
struggled silently to cross his toes.

A minute passed, and another, and then,
just as it seemed that Deathwing, Lord of

the Skies wasn't interested in the pile of fruit, he suddenly and greedily swooped onto it. Immediately, Dad reared up from behind the buddleia, grinning fiercely, and yanked as hard as he could on the twine. The toasting fork flew up into the air, Deathwing, Lord of the Skies flew up into the netting, and Dad, yelling loudly, flung himself forwards. The falling toasting fork struck him on the head, and he plunged full-length into the netting with a noise of despair.

The other Quigleys ran out from their hiding place. Dad was struggling in the netting. Quite a lot of him was covered in fruit. The hoolah hoop was bent in half and the toasting fork was sticking out of the buddleia.

'Did I get him?' Dad panted, rubbing mango from his face.

They looked in the netting, which was empty except for Dad. They looked round the garden. Deathwing, Lord of the Skies was nowhere to be seen.

In the moment of silence that followed, Will said, 'Listen.'

*Tuckle, tuckle, natter, natter, natter.*

They all looked up, even Dad, who had got the mango out of his eyes, and they saw Deathwing, Lord of the Skies sitting in the lowest branches of the chestnut tree.

Then an absolutely astonishing thing

happened. Will left the others and walked towards the budgie very slowly, holding his finger out, and talking in a quiet conversational voice.

'Come on, Deathwing. Come on, boy. Come on, Deathboy.' He whistled softly, and talked. 'It's all right. Come on now.' Almost immediately, Deathwing, Lord of the Skies flew down with a small screech and landed on his finger, and Will gently took hold of him.

From his position on the lawn, Dad gagged.

'But,' he said, choking. 'But. But that's exactly what I was trying to do.'

On Sunday morning, the Quigleys sat in the back room eating their breakfast in their pyjamas and dressing gowns. In their cage on top of the toy cupboard the budgies were having their breakfast too. They went *tuckle, tuckle, natter, natter, natter.*

Dad sat with his swollen ankle up on a stool. He felt very tired.

'When I've finished breakfast,' Will said, 'I'm going to train the budgies to talk.'

Behind his paper, Dad moaned to himself.

Will ignored him. 'They know me now. We understand each other. I'm going to talk to them about things.' He thought for a moment. 'I might ask them what they think of you leaving that window open.'

Dad limped with the paper into the front room. He had nearly fallen asleep when Will came in.

'Well,' Will said. 'That didn't take long.'

Dad looked at him suspiciously. 'What do you mean?'

'Told you I was going to teach them to talk. Well, it didn't take me long.'

Disbelieving, Dad followed him into the back room, where Mum and Lucy were standing looking at the cage. Will got Deathwing, Lord of the Skies out and held him on his finger. Deathwing, Lord of the Skies was strangely calm, quite unlike normal.

'Hello,' Will said. The bird cocked his head on one side.

'Hello,' Will said in a deeper voice. Deathwing, Lord of the Skies shook his head feathers and looked interested.

'Hello,' Will said in an even deeper, more tragic voice. 'Hello. Hel-lowww.'

'Hello, Ralphie,' the budgie said brightly.

Dad staggered sideways, broke the family

rules, and Mum told him off.

'You see,' Will said, beaming. 'He knows my name.'

Dad frowned. 'But he didn't say your name,' he said. 'He said, "Hello, Ralphie."'

'No, he didn't, he said "Hello, Willie."'

'Sounded like Ralphie to me.'

Will scowled so hard his forehead seemed to cover his eyes. 'Typical,' he said. 'I spend all morning teaching him to talk, and all you can do is criticize.'

Dad apologized. He said he was going to go for a walk in the park and, out of pure kindness, Lucy said she'd go with him.

It was a clear blue cool day. Lucy and Dad walked down the street holding hands. Sometimes Lucy didn't like holding hands, but today she thought Dad wanted to.

'Amazing,' Dad kept saying, shaking his head. 'Just amazing.'

They went down Parkside Road, and turned into the path that led to the park.

'Look,' Lucy said. 'Someone's done a picture of Deathwing, Lord of the Skies.'

They stopped and looked at the picture fastened to a lamppost.

'Why have they done a picture of Deathwing, Lord of the Skies?' Lucy said.

'It's a good picture, isn't it? It looks just like him.'

Dad stared at the picture. 'Listen to this, Poodle,' he said in a strange voice. 'It says: "Have you seen this bird? Green budgerigar, very tame and friendly. Lost on Friday. Will come to your hand, and answers

36

to the name of Ralphie." And then there's a phone number.'

'Ralphie,' Lucy said. 'That's funny. That's what Deathwing, Lord of the Skies said.'

Dad looked at her. 'Oh dear,' he said.

'Isn't it Deathwing, Lord of the Skies?' Lucy said. 'Is it Ralphie?'

They turned together and walked back up Parkside Road. 'Oh dear,' Dad kept saying.

As they went in, Will was standing in the back room with the green budgerigar on his finger. He said, 'It's very odd, Dad. I've taught him to talk all right, but he seems to have this speech problem.'

After they had taken Ralphie back to his owners, the Quigleys sat in the front room and comforted Will. Lucy did him a picture of Deathwing, Lord of the Skies which she said he could put up on the lampposts now that the pictures of Ralphie had been taken down.

Will shook his head. 'No point,' he said. 'He'll be halfway to Singapore by now.'

Dad blushed.

'It's all right,' Will said heavily. 'I knew it was too good to be true when he flew onto my finger. He was always too stupid to do that.'

They sat quietly for a while, and then it was time for Will to practise the piano.

'At least the piano got fixed,' he said. 'So something good happened yesterday.'

He sat at the piano, looking at his hands and sighing, and then he began to practise. After a while he stopped.

'I don't think much of that piano tuner,' he said. 'It doesn't sound right.'

He played on for a bit, making quite a lot of mistakes.

'This piano sounds awful,' he said.

'Come on now,' Mum said. 'Don't take it out on the piano, just because you're upset.' She went to sit next to him.

Will made a mistake, and then another.

'You see,' he said. 'The notes keep

missing and they don't sound right.'

'Try it again,' Mum said. 'Hit the keys firmly.'

Will hit the keys firmly and the piano squawked. Mum and Will looked at each other, amazed. Will flung open the piano lid, and Deathwing, Lord of the Skies burst madly and loudly into the room.

The Quigleys found themselves standing up and speaking together.

'The piano tuner left the lid up,' Dad said.

'And he flew into the piano,' Mum said.

'And I put the lid down again without realizing,' Dad said.

'So he didn't fly out of the window at all,' Will said.

'And I *am* stupid,' Dad said.

There was a slight silence after this.

'I think I should play "Sing, Bird, Sing",' Lucy said kindly, and she did.

'And Deathwing, Lord of the Skies isn't stupid after all,' Will added.

They looked up at him flying in mad circles round the ceiling.

'Well,' Will said. 'Not totally stupid.'

# Will in a Dream

# Will in a Dream

Mum and Dad said Will was too dreamy. They said he forgot things, and didn't pay attention, and left things behind, and didn't think. They were sitting in the back room one Sunday, talking about it. Or rather, Mum and Dad were talking about it, and Will was reading *The Beano*.

'I hope you haven't lost your new coat,' Mum said. 'It's not on the pegs.'

Will carried on reading *The Beano*, grinning to himself.

'Will!'

'What?'

'Where is it?'

'Where's what?'

'Where's your new coat?'

Will looked at the coat pegs and back at

Mum. 'Well, it's not on the pegs,' he said. He saw the look on her face. 'But I know where it is,' he went on in a different, more helpful voice. 'I know *exactly* where it is.'

Mum waited for him to say something else, but he didn't. He went back to *The Beano*.

'Well, where?' she asked at last.

'What? Oh. At school.'

'Are you sure?'

'Yes.'

'You're absolutely sure?'

'Yes, I told you.' He resumed reading *The Beano*. 'Unless it's at Tim's,' he said after a moment.

Mum opened her mouth with a bit of a hiss, and Will looked up. 'Or Dani's,' he added. 'There's a sort of very small chance it might be at Dani's. But basically I do know where it is, so that's all right. Oh, and shall I clear away the breakfast things?'

Will had noticed that when he offered to do something helpful, it often made Mum and Dad forget what they were talking about. Today it didn't work. Mum had that squeezed look. It was not her worst look, but it was one of her worst. It came somewhere between the distracted look and the bone-munching look of fury. Mum's squeezed look was difficult to make go away.

'You don't look after your things,' Mum said crossly. 'I bet your friends don't treat their things like this, do they?'

Will thought it best to agree, and he shook his head sadly.

Dad weighed in. 'I bet your friends aren't always leaving things at school, are they?' he said.

Will shook his head again, looking mournful.

'I really don't know what we're doing wrong,' Dad sighed, and Will was just wondering how to answer this when Mum suddenly asked him if he'd given out all the invitations to his birthday party at school. That took him by surprise.

'What invitations?' he said, before he could stop himself.

They discovered them all still in his school bag, and it seemed as if Mum's squeezed look was about to be replaced by her bone-munching one.

Will thought quickly. 'I'll take them now,' he said. 'I don't mind. I'll enjoy it.' Mum still looked quite fierce. 'It'll be good for me,' he added. 'I can put Tim's through his letterbox, and Matt's, and Sandy's, and I can cycle over to Dani's with his. That's almost half of them.'

Mum and Dad calmed down. 'OK,' Mum said. 'But be back by lunchtime.'

Will put the invitations in his pocket and

went to the door.

'Oh. And can I stay at Dani's for a bit, to play? If I promise to come back on time?' He smiled sweetly. It was a smile he had practised in the mirror. He wasn't sure if Mum and Dad could see the sweet smile all the way from the back room, but he thought it was worth it anyway.

'All right,' Mum said. 'But make sure you're back by one o'clock.' She used a firm voice. 'Don't get in a dream and forget.'

Will turned to go.

'Don't forget!' Dad called. He used an even firmer voice. 'Don't get in a dream!'

'Course I won't,' Will called back. His voice was not at all firm.

He went up and down the street delivering invitations. It was a fine warm spring morning, blue and gold. The front gardens were full of lilacs and azaleas and Yellow Betty. The Quigleys' rose bush, heavy with

buds, hung over their front wall. Soon the
blind lady who lived at number thirty-six
would be asking them to cut it back so she
didn't walk into it. Will liked the blind lady.
He liked her guide dog too. The dog was
spectacularly badly behaved. Sometimes, if
the Quigleys had left their front door open,
it would come bounding curiously into their
house and romp around the kitchen, while
the blind lady cursed it loudly from the
pavement. Will hoped he might bump into the
blind lady and her dog on his way to Dani's.

The gutters of the back roads were filled
with fallen cherry blossom. He went along
the cycle track that ran between the lake
and the vicarage, and into the park. He
didn't see the blind lady or her dog. At the
other side of the park he went across the
wooden bridge, and turned into the road
where school was.

Suddenly he stopped. The school gates
were wide open, and the main door was
open too. He frowned. School ought to be
closed on Sundays. He looked up and down

the empty street, then back at the school buildings. Leaning forward on his bike, he listened. He could hear noises. Something was going on inside. He asked himself what it could be. Had burglars broken in to steal the valuable chalk or rare guinea pigs? Could dark forces have taken over the school for their own secret purposes? Or perhaps Miss Strickland had been involved in some sort of accident. He liked that particularly. He imagined Mr Sheringham rushing into the car park, shouting, 'Quick, four strong men! She's fallen down!'

Then, for no reason at all, he remembered his coat. He really did think he'd left it at school. It would be hanging on the peg outside his classroom. He could nip in and fetch it while school was open. What a surprise Mum and Dad would have when he came home wearing his lost coat. The thought of it was almost as nice as the thought of Miss Strickland's accident.

He got off his bike and chained it to the railings. There was another bike chained up a bit further along, and a woolly hat stuck on top of the gate. It was just like some people to leave their things behind. He went cautiously across the yard to the door, and peeped in. There was no one in sight. After a moment he slipped inside.

He'd never been in school at the weekend before; it felt empty and quiet, not like proper school at all. There was no one in the school office, so he went down the corridor, his footsteps echoing as he walked. He went into the hall and stood there looking round. Usually the hall was packed and noisy; now it was hushed and still. He noticed things he didn't usually see: the rocking chair in the corner and the orange girders across the ceiling. He sniffed. There was a smell of polish. The wooden floor, usually greyish, was glossy.

Was it the stillness, or the quietness, or the smell of polish that made him go into a dream? In his dream he saw the hall filling up with people for assembly, teachers

leading their classes in, and the children filing in behind, and he saw Mr Sheringham come through the door, and with him all his friends, some of them jostling and some of them whispering, and Sandy tripping up Dani, and Tim treading on Matt's toes, and, right at the end, a blond-haired boy with freckles – himself, Will Quigley, gazing round and chewing a fingernail.

He came out of his dream when he heard the noises again. Voices and music. Where were they coming from? Going out of the hall, he went quietly down the deserted corridor, following the sounds and feeling daring. Past the guinea pigs, past the girls' toilets, across the display area covered with pictures of Ancient Greeks being turned to stone by the Gorgon's head, down the corridor to Miss Petz's classroom. Now he could hear what the sounds were: people talking – not children, but adults. The door to the classroom was ajar, so he tiptoed up and peeped in.

Some men were standing round the piano. He recognized Ben, Tim's dad. He didn't know the others. They were shuffling papers and talking. Will guessed it was some sort of choir practice. As he watched, one of the men said, 'OK, from the top,' and they all straightened up, held the papers in front of them, and stared at the wall behind the piano, looking very serious. 'After four,' the man said.

Will had never seen Ben sing before. It was staggeringly funny. One second he was a perfectly normal man with pale hair and a mild face, and the next he was a pop-eyed lunatic who'd just stepped on a tack. Will retreated, cramming his hands into his mouth. He knew he shouldn't laugh. Certainly he shouldn't laugh out loud or he would be discovered. For several minutes he rolled on the floor biting his knuckles and jabbing his fingers into his cheeks, and

squeezing his nostrils shut so the laugh wouldn't explode out of his nose until, at last, the fit passed and he lolled against the wall, grinning soundlessly. And it was then, with some surprise, that he remembered his coat again.

He set off happily towards Mr Sheringham's classroom.

It was nice being in school with no one else around, just being curious and a bit dreamy. He thought the dreaminess had something to do with the stillness. Or perhaps it was the warmth. The sun was coming in the windows of the new block in fuzzy golden shafts. He waltzed down the corridor humming to himself until his classroom came in sight, and then, for the first time, it crossed his mind that perhaps his coat wouldn't be there after all. At once his heart beat high up in his chest, and he began to think things to make it be there. If it's there, he thought, I'll be nice to Lucy tomorrow. At least part of tomorrow, until lunchtime, say. And I'll clean the budgies out. I might even clean them out twice.

He thought that was enough, so he stopped thinking, and went carefully down the corridor until he came to his peg. And on his peg was his coat. He smelled it to make sure it was his, and put it on, and grinned to himself. His thinking had worked. Sometimes it did. Now he'd show Mum and Dad whether he knew where his coat was or not. It was turning out to be a very good Sunday morning indeed.

Before he left, he peeped into his empty classroom through the window in the door. It was filled with sunshine, and dust swam in the yellow light. He looked at his desk, where he sat every day. It seemed different without him, smaller and more like the other desks, and he felt sort of sorry for it.

Though it was warm, he zipped up his coat so he could feel it round him, and went down the other corridor. On his way he passed the lost property box. It really was amazing how much stuff people left behind, huge piles of things. There was a red wool coat that had been in the box for ages, and a pair of yellow trousers and about seventeen shoes, all different, and a great purple shirt-thing so big and appalling it must surely have been Miss Strickland's. When he put it on, it came down to his ankles. He put the yellow trousers on too, to have something to tuck the shirt-thing into, and then he thought he might as well put on some of the shoes. There was a fur sleeveless jacket he thought would make a good hat, though in fact it wasn't as good as a silver plastic skirt which fitted very snugly round his ears.

He wasn't sure how long he'd been dressing up when he noticed the silence. Before, there had always been faint noises coming from Miss Petz's classroom, where Ben's choir was practising. Now he couldn't hear them. He removed the silver plastic skirt from his head to listen better. No, there

were no noises at all. The whole school was perfectly hushed. He glanced nervously up and down the empty corridor. It looked less friendly than before. For the first time, it seemed somehow wrong that he was there. He thought to himself that he ought to go before it was too late. And it was then that he heard the footsteps.

At first he thought perhaps they weren't real footsteps. Sometimes, when he was nervous, he imagined noises that weren't there. But, as he listened, the footsteps came nearer.

He crouched down and tried to blend in with the lost property box, which he very nearly did because he was wearing so much of it. He began to think things to make the footsteps stop, really big things like, I'll be nice to Lucy the whole of tomorrow and all next week, if only this isn't happening. But it was no good. The footsteps came slowly nearer. And finally, as he watched, a figure came round the corner.

'Peachey!' Will cried.

The boy in the corridor jumped and looked all round and shouted, 'I didn't do it! I wasn't even thinking of it!'

Will stood up and waved. 'Over here, Tim!'

Tim stared at Will in horror.

'It's me!' Will called.

Tim recognized him and rushed down the corridor. 'Watch out,' he panted as he ran. 'There's someone else in here. He just shouted out. Sort of low and horrible. Vicious and low and horrible and vicious.'

Will realized with surprise that Tim was a bigger dreamer than he was.

'Tim,' he said. 'That was me.'

61

Tim thought about this. After a while he said, 'Why are you dressed like that?'

'Like what?'

'Like a jumble sale.'

Will took off the lost property, which he had forgotten about. 'I left my coat, so I came in to get it,' he explained. 'And then I sort of got carried away. What are you doing here?'

'Left my bag. I was going past, and I saw the door open, and I came in.'

They were so pleased they hugged each other.

'Your dad's here,' Will said. 'Or, at least, he was.'

Tim was uninterested in this. 'He thought I didn't know where my bag was,' he said with disgust.

Will nodded. 'They didn't believe I knew where my coat was.'

'They never believe you. That's one of the things about them.'

They walked along the corridor towards the hall.

'How long have you been here?' Will asked.

'About half an hour.'

'What have you been doing?'

'I went upstairs and played with the fire extinguisher for a bit. I wasn't going to steal it, I didn't even think of it. Anyway,' he added, 'I couldn't get it off the wall. What about you?'

'Same sort of stuff,' Will said. 'I watched your dad singing. That was good, his mouth's much bigger than I thought. It's a good mouth,' he added, in case Tim thought he was being rude. 'Oh, yes, I got my coat too, I keep forgetting that. And then it got quiet,' he said.

Tim nodded. 'I don't like things this quiet.'

Will said, 'I can't hear any singing at all, can you? Maybe they're having a rest.'

They listened. The school seemed very big and empty all around them. Bigger and emptier than before. They walked close together.

'Weren't the doors to the hall open when we came in?' Tim said, when they got to the end of the corridor.

'Someone's shut them,' Will said.

They looked at each other.

'Do you think your dad's still here?'

'I don't know.'

'Do you think *anyone's* here?'

They began to walk faster. They jogged through the hall, then ran from the hall to the main door, and when they got to it they found that it was locked.

They stood panting, looking through the

glass panel at the yard.

Will sighed. 'Now I'm going to be late home,' he said. 'And I promised I wouldn't be.'

Tim pulled at the door handles and gave the door a kicking, and when he was tired, he said, 'We're locked in. We're going to be locked in all day,' he said. 'And all night,' he added.

If Will had been on his own, he would have been frightened. But he had Tim with him, and he knew straightaway that it was very important not to be frightened, so as to be able to think of a plan.

'It's OK,' he said. 'We just have to think of a plan.'

'I don't like plans much,' Tim said. He began to kick the door again.

'Wait,' Will said. 'I know. We can phone my mum and dad. There's a phone in the office.'

They ran together to the office, and when they got there they found that door locked as well.

'I'm going to go back to the main door,' Tim said, 'to see what happens if I kick it a bit more.'

'No, wait,' Will said. 'I know something else we can do. We can climb out of a window.'

Tim liked that, but the nearest window wouldn't open.

'It's locked too,' he said. 'These catches won't move.'

'Let's try another one,' Will said. 'They can't all be locked. I mean, there are hundreds of windows in this school. Who would go around locking them all?'

They tried thirty-seven windows, and they were all locked.

'I've thought of a plan now,' Tim said. 'We can smash a window. That'll open it.'

Will looked doubtful. 'Well, I don't think I'd actually want to smash one,' he said.

'I would,' Tim said.

'But, Tim, we don't know how to smash windows.'

'It's pretty easy. You have to be careful to knock out all the jagged bits afterwards so you don't cut your wrists off. But then you just climb through.'

He began to tap expertly round the edges of the window pane. Will realized he was serious. 'Easy, Tim,' he said. 'Tim?'

'What?'

'I don't think I've told you before that I don't like loud noises.'

'Stand back.' Tim rolled up his sleeves, looked at his wrists, then rolled his sleeves down again.

'And we could get into trouble, Tim. Our names could go in the book.'

Tim didn't say anything, he was too busy taking off his football socks and putting them on his hand to make a sort of boxing glove. He took a deep breath and began to swing his arm round and round.

Will put his fingers in his ears and closed his eyes.

When he opened them again, Tim was tottering up and down the corridor, holding his hand in front of him, very red in the face. He had taken the socks off his hand, and his hand was very red too. The window wasn't broken, though there was a

sort of smudge in the middle of it.

Will went over to Tim and patted him on the shoulder. 'Never mind, Tim,' he said. He used a sympathetic voice that reminded him of Dad. 'You hit it really hard, I couldn't have hit it that hard. It's not your fault it didn't break. In fact, I think I remember someone telling me all the windows in this school were made with special glass from Russia which you actually can't break. It's unbreakable.' He felt very relieved.

When Tim had finished crying, he wiped his face with his socks and began to look around. 'All I need is a brick,' he said. 'A brick or an iron bar, or maybe a metal chair, to throw through it.'

'Wait a minute,' Will said suddenly. 'What's that noise?'

They listened.

'Voices,' Will said. 'Outside. Quick!'

They crowded to the glass panels of the doors, and looked out onto the road.

'Look, it's Dani and Sandy!' Tim said.

Their friends were walking along the pavement. They saw Dani run across the grass verge to the school railings where the other bike was chained up.

'Here it is!' they heard him call to Sandy. 'I told them I knew where it was. They wouldn't believe me.'

'And here's my hat,' they heard Sandy shout back. 'They said it was lost for good. Now I'll show them.'

'Look,' Dani said. 'Someone else has left their bike here. People leave their stuff everywhere.'

'Hey!' Will and Tim shouted together. 'Hey!'

Dani and Sandy looked up and down the road.

'In here!' Tim and Will shouted.

When Dani and Sandy saw them, there was terrific excitement all round. Dani and Sandy climbed the railings and jumped up and down outside, and Tim gave the door another kicking, and Will showed Dani and Sandy how Tim had punched the window and hurt his fist and had to go and sit down.

When they'd all calmed down, Sandy asked if they were coming out to play.

'We're locked in, you idiot,' Tim said.

'Oh,' Sandy said. 'I thought you were just pretending.'

'Chill, boys,' Dani said. 'We'll rescue you.' He was very calm. He wasn't locked in.

'How?' Will said.

They were all silent for a while.

'What about tunnelling?' Sandy said. 'I saw this film once.'

Dani retreated a little way and scanned the school front. 'Boys,' he said. 'It's really quite simple. Just leave it to me.'

Sandy gave him a leg up to the window sill, and Dani clung to the wall. After a while he fell off.

'What were you trying to do?' Will asked.

Dani explained that if only he could get hold of the guttering, he could pull himself onto the porch roof, climb up the roof to the top, swing across to a nearby window, heave himself up onto the main roof and search for a skylight, which it would be easy to smash his way through.

They all considered this plan. Eventually Will said that they were trying to get out, not Dani get in.

Sandy said he thought explosives would be useful. 'I saw this film once,' he said. 'And they made dynamite by weeing on this grey stuff.'

For half an hour they thought up plans, and Tim occasionally kicked the door, and Dani tried five times to get beyond the window sill, and finally Sandy said, 'Oh well, I don't think anything we do is going to work. I'll go home and get the key off my mum.'

There was a pause after he said this.

'What do you mean, "get the key"?' Will said.

'Mum's chairperson of the school governors,' Sandy said. 'And she has to organize meetings after school and stuff. So, of course you have to have a key if you do that sort of thing.'

'Oh.' There was a vague air of disappointment.

'Unless anyone can think of something else,' Sandy said.

Nobody could. Sandy went.

When he returned with his mum, everything seemed to speed up again. She unlocked the door and Will and Tim bounded out as if newly released to the wild, and all four boys leaped around the yard, whooping and telling each other what had just happened, even though they had all been there and knew it all already.

Then Will suddenly said, 'Hang on. What's the time?'

'One o'clock,' Sandy's mum said.

Will slapped his forehead. 'I'm going to be late, and I promised I wouldn't be!' He ran for his bike.

He went at top speed down the road and across the wooden bridge, and down the cycle track by the vicarage, and into Parkside Road, and down the road to his house, almost without breathing, and flung himself through his front door.

'Here I am!' he shouted, when he could.

Lucy came into the hall. 'Are you late?' she asked.

'No,' Will said casually, panting.

Mum came into the hall, looking at her watch.

'Not very,' he added. Mum was staring at him, and Dad came down the stairs, looking distracted.

'Good God,' Dad said.

'What?' Will asked nervously.

'Well. I didn't think we'd see that again.'

'You *did* know where it was, all along,' Mum said.

For a moment he was confused. Then he remembered his coat, which he was wearing, and his whole face went pleased.

'Oh yes,' he said, and his voice slowed down and had a sort of a grin to it. 'Told you I knew where it was. I mean, it's all to do with not forgetting things and not getting into a dream, isn't it?'

Both Mum and Dad were smiling and shaking their heads as he swaggered past them into the kitchen.

'By the way, did you have a good time?' Dad asked.

'Pretty good,' Will said. 'All things considering.'

'Good boy,' Mum said. 'And you gave Dani his invitation?'

Will turned. 'What invitation?' he said.

# Mum at the Fête

# Mum at the Fête

Mum had her wisdom teeth out. She came home from the hospital carrying them in a little plastic bag. They looked like dice with legs.

'Sick,' Lucy said.

Will was interested in how much Mum was going to get from the tooth fairy.

'I don't think fairies deal in such large amounts of tooth,' Dad said. 'What we really need are people who deal in black market ivory.'

Mum said she felt fine, but Dad was worried about her and said she had to spend a couple of days in bed. 'Peace and rest,' he said. 'Having your wisdom teeth out is a serious operation.' He told the children that they had to be quiet in the house for the next two days. He had that determined look, the slightly cross-eyed one.

'Two days?' Mum said. 'What am I going to do with myself for two whole days?'

'Nothing,' Dad said. 'That's the point. We're going to do everything.'

Will and Lucy took it in turns to carry orange squash up to her. They took her twelve beakers of squash on the first day, and fifteen beakers on the second, so as to cheer her up. She didn't look cheered up. She looked bored.

'I'm definitely going to get up for the school fête on Saturday,' she said.

Dad said he'd think about it. In the meantime he did what Mum usually did. He took Will and Lucy to school, and picked them up from school, and gave them tea, and gave Lucy's friends tea, and gave Will's friends tea, and took Lucy to her ballet lesson, and took Will to his clarinet lesson, and did Lucy's spellings with her, and helped Will with his science revision, and made Lucy's packed lunch, and unstitched the piece of shapeless towel that Will had been working on at school for four weeks and turned it into a Tudor hat, which is what it was supposed to be.

'I liked it the way it was,' Will said.

Will and Lucy thought Dad was taking things too far. It was hard for them, being calm and quiet all the time.

On Thursday night they fooled around when they were getting into bed, and Dad got cross. 'Quiet!' he whispered fiercely, tucking them in. 'Mum's probably asleep.'

They fooled a bit more. Dad hissed
again.

Will thrust his finger up to Dad's face.
'Look at that,' he said. There was a small
dark ball of something on the end of one of
his fingers.

Dad recoiled. 'What is
it?'

'Bloody snot,' Will said
with satisfaction.

Dad expressed his disgust,
so Will flicked it onto the
carpet.

'What did you do that
for?' Dad said furiously.

Lucy scrambled over.
'Where is it?' she said
excitedly. 'Where did it go?'

'For God's sake!' Dad
yelled. 'You have to be
quiet!'

Mum appeared at the top of the attic
stairs, looking interested. 'What was it?' she
asked. 'Where did it go?'

Dad sent her back to bed.

The next night it was the same. Will and Lucy had been quiet ever since they came in from school, and by bedtime they didn't have any more quietness in them.

'Hey, Dad!' Will said from the top bunk. 'Do you know what I learned today? I learned to sing in Hebrew.'

'No, Will!' Dad said, but Will had already wrapped himself in his duvet and begun to sway from side to side, singing in a loud but tragically low voice, 'Dosh, mosh, kabbosh . . .' and Dad shouted so hard he said afterwards he thought he'd damaged his throat.

Upstairs they heard Mum laughing.

On Saturday, the day of the school fête, Mum woke early and said that she would make pancakes for breakfast, and Dad said, 'No.' Even though he was feeling tired after doing everything that Mum usually did, he got up and went down to make the pancakes himself.

The first pancake burned and Dad tossed it fairly accurately into the bin. The second one burned and he missed the bin. The third got tangled up and looked like knickers, and Dad gave it to Will.

'This isn't a pancake,' Will said.

'What is it then?' Dad said sharply.

Will thought hard. He found it difficult to describe the knicker-pancake-thing. 'It's a lump of despair,' he said at last.

After they had cleared the table and thrown away the frying pan, they practised skipping, because Lucy had entered the skipping competition at the school fête. She was going to do it with her best friend, Pokehead.

'Can Mum come down and practise with me?' Lucy asked.

'I know skipping,' Dad said. 'I know all about skipping. I was skipping champion twelve times on the trot when I was younger.'

Lucy frowned at him.

'Twelve,' Dad said. 'Or was it thirteen?'

He tied one end of a spare piece of electric flex to the radiator in the back room, and turned the other end.

'You have to sing the song as well,' Lucy said. 'Do you know the song *'Two Six Nine'*?'

'I know it all right,' Dad said. 'You jump, I'll sing.'

He turned the electric flex, and Lucy jumped, and Dad sang:

*Two six nine*
*The goose drank wine*
*The cow danced a jig and the*
*fish went blind.*

Lucy stopped jumping. 'Those aren't the words,' she said crossly, and at that moment Mum came into the room. She was dressed and looked very well, and she took the electric flex from Dad, who didn't say anything.

'Are you ready?' Mum said to Lucy. And, as she turned the flex, she began to sing in a loud, clear voice:

*Two six nine*
*The goose drank wine*
*The monkey chewed tobacco on the*
*street car line.*
*The line broke*
*The monkey got a choke*
*And they all went to heaven in a*
*little row boat.*

They practised it eight times with great energy and skill, laughing and clapping.

'Well, I suppose you're up now,' Dad said to Mum. He was lying down on the sofa, looking tired. 'I must say, you're pretty good at this skipping thing.'

'Mum's good at the old words,' Lucy said. 'But she doesn't know the new words that Pokehead and I will have to know. I mean, when you were skipping, Mum, it was a long time ago.' She looked very kind so Mum would know she wasn't being rude.

The phone rang and Lucy ran to answer it. She liked answering the phone; she liked asking people who they wanted to speak to, and liked the little things you say in between the other things, like 'How are you?' and 'Yes, I'm fine.' But when she came back after answering the phone this time, she was crying.

'What's the matter, Poodlefish?' Mum said.

'Pokehead can't be my partner any more,' Lucy said.

'Why not?' Mum said.

'She's hurt her arm. And now I won't be able to do the skipping competition.'

All the Quigleys were quiet, even though Dad didn't tell them to be.

'Everyone else will be doing it,' Lucy said, trying not to cry. 'But I won't be able to because I've got no one to do it with!'

'Don't worry, Lucy,' Mum said. She used a very determined voice. 'We'll find you another partner.' She did determined much better than Dad.

Mum was on the phone for an hour talking to other mums, but at lunchtime she still hadn't found anyone to be Lucy's partner. All Lucy's other friends had partners already.

'Never mind, Poodlefish,' Dad said. 'I'm sure we'll find someone once we get to the fête.' Dad's voice wasn't determined. It was sort of vague.

Saturday afternoon was bright and warm, and the school playing-field was full of people wandering round the stalls and tents and games. It was a very good fête. On the field there was a clown, a football competition, an international food tent, a white elephant stall, a Samba band, a barbecue, a coconut shy, a place where you could have your face painted and all sorts of other stalls and games. Inside the school there was a café and an amusement arcade.

'What we have to do first,' Mum said, 'is find a partner for Lucy in the skipping competition. Agreed?'

They agreed.

'What we have to do next,' Dad said, 'is look after Mum. She's still not very strong. She mustn't do anything too tiring, like games and things. Do you agree?'

They all agreed, except Mum.

'Where *is* Mum?' Lucy said, looking round.

They saw her across the field laughing with a group of other mums, and Dad

made hand signs to her which she couldn't
possibly understand. Anyway, she turned
her back before he'd finished.

'This is going to be hard,' Will said. 'She
looks pretty perky to me.' And then they all
went off round the fête.

Will found Tim. After Tim had said that
he didn't want to be Lucy's skipping
partner, they had a go on the tombola, and
Tim won a set of wooden hairbrushes,
which he dropped into a man's pocket
because he hated having his hair brushed.
Will said that Tim shouldn't have done
that, and Tim said the man would probably
be glad of new hairbrushes, and Will said
he probably wouldn't because he was as
bald as a coot.

That cheered them up, and they went over to the football competition.

Suddenly Will rushed forward, shouting, 'Mum! No!'

Mum was standing in front of the goal, just about to take her first penalty. Will got to her as she took it, and the ball left her foot at an angle of 70 degrees and broke a branch in an overhead tree, which fell with a crash, narrowly missing the goalkeeper.

'I want that again,' Mum said to the man in charge.

Will said, 'You're not allowed. You're not allowed games and things. Dad said. She's not,' he said to the man. 'She's too weak.'

The man looked balefully at the broken branch.

Mum went, looking fed up, and Will took the rest of her penalties.

'There's something wrong with this ball,' he said afterwards.

Tim had a go. He wasn't as good as Will, but he had more tricks. For his first

penalty, he dashed up to the ball as if about
to kick it with his right foot, and at the last
second thrashed it with his left, and it went
in off the goalkeeper's forehead. For his
second, he dashed up to the ball, and at the

95

last second stopped, clutching his knee in agony, and when the keeper came out of

his goal, saying, 'Are you OK?', he suddenly straightened up and gave the ball a terrific thrash, and it went in off the keeper's nose.

The third and final penalty he missed. They tried to make him go into the churchyard to get the ball back but he wouldn't.

'This is a very good fête,' Will said. 'Look, there's my dad on the rowing machine game.'

They went over. Dad was sitting on the machine, smiling to himself. 'I used to row on a machine just like this,' he said dreamily. Next to the machine there was a blackboard with names and different times written on it.

'Look,' Will said. 'Someone called Ted's done it in fifty-eight seconds. You could do it in less than fifty-eight seconds. I bet you could.'

Dad paid his money, and the lady in charge said, 'Go!' and Dad gave an

enormous grunt and shot forwards as if he'd
been kicked in the buttocks. He went
forwards and backwards, hissing and
heaving, and the veins in his neck stood
out, and his face turned an astonishing
purple which Will had never seen before. It
was a wonderful sight.

'One minute, fifteen seconds,' the lady
said. 'Very good for someone your age.
Teas are being served in the hall.'

'Are you sure this machine's working
properly?' Dad asked her, when he could.

Will and Tim drifted away. 'Don't forget to stop Mum doing any games,' Dad shouted after them, still panting. 'She's not strong enough.'

Lucy thought it was a very good fête too. There were lots of her friends there, and every time she met one of them she asked if they would be her skipping partner, but they always said no. Sometimes they were already someone else's partner, sometimes they didn't want to skip. Lucy knew that some of the girls she asked were rubbish at skipping, but even they said no. It was depressing. But she met Pokehead, who had her arm in a sling, and they went round the fête together.

'How did you hurt your arm?' Lucy asked.

'Because of Tim getting his head stuck in the bannisters.'

'Did your arm get stuck too?'

'No,' Pokehead said. 'Just Tim's head. We put Vaseline on it. To pull him out more smoothly. I like Vaseline, don't you?'

'Yes,' Lucy said. 'So, did you hurt your arm pulling him out?'

'No,' Pokehead said. 'When he got his head out he kicked me and I fell down the stairs.'

'Oh, I see,' Lucy said. 'That wasn't very nice,' she added.

'Well, he didn't like me putting the Vaseline up his nose.'

They went to the clothes stall and bought a pair of spotted pants so big they could both get into them at the same time, and

they were just going to have a go on the ping-pong ball game and win a goldfish they could share, when, to Pokehead's surprise, Lucy suddenly ran off, shouting, 'Mum! No!'

Mum was lining up to take part in the tug-of-war. She scowled when she saw Lucy running towards her.

'I'm just helping them set up,' she said.

'No you're not,' Lucy said. 'You're about to do tugging, and you're not allowed. Dad said.'

The man in charge, who was just about to blow the whistle, shouted at them, 'Your team has one too many!'

'You have to go, Lucy,' Mum said.

'No, Mum,' Lucy said. '*You* have to go.'

Some of Lucy's friends were in the team, and they turned round and looked at Mum, and then at Lucy. 'We want Lucy,' they said. 'Mums can't pull as hard.' And Mum, looking very fed up, went.

At the white elephant stall she met Will and Tim. Will looked secretive. His trouser pockets were full of something.

'I've always had an eye for a bargain,' he said. 'Ask Dad.'

Mum remembered Will's bargains from other fêtes. They littered the Quigleys' house – a china dog with its left ear missing, an ashtray in the shape of a canoe with 'Present from Niagara Falls' written on the side, a wooden corkscrew decorated with the crest of Ostend.

'Where *is* Dad?' Mum said.

'On the rowing machine again,' Will said.

'What do you mean, "again"?'

'He says there's something wrong with it,' Will said. 'He asked the lady to see if she could fix it.'

'Is he all right?'

'Dunno. He looked a bit grey last time I saw him. Someone called Ted can do it in fifty-eight seconds.'

It was a beautiful summer day. A jazz band began to play. The Quigleys were having a very good time, though Lucy still didn't have a skipping partner, and Mum was doing things which she wasn't strong enough to do, and Dad was looking grey.

'Hello,' Mum said to Dad when he came up to her. 'You look a bit grey. Have you beaten Ted yet?'

'It shifts,' he said. His voice was very quiet. 'The whole machine wobbles. I hope

you're taking it easy,' he added weakly.
'Why don't we go and get a cup of tea?'

Mum looked shifty. 'Not just now,' she said.

'Why not?'

'I'll come in a minute.'

Suddenly there was a loud voice out of the
air saying, 'Ready, ladies? On your marks!'

For the first time Dad realized that Mum
was standing in a row of other mums at the
white line at the end of the athletics track.
When they heard the voice, some of the
mums crouched down, looking serious.

'Get set!' the voice said.

'Wait!' Dad said, and he put his hand on
Mum's arm.

The voice out of the air said, 'Go!' and
all the other mums sprinted down the
athletics track in the mum's race. 'It was
very lucky I came along just then,' Dad
said. 'You could have worn yourself out
doing that.' He coughed once or twice.
'Anyway, I think I'll just have one more go
rowing,' he said.

As he left, Will and Lucy came up, and

the three of them went to the café.

'Have you found anyone to be your skipping partner?' Mum said to Lucy.

Lucy shook her head.

'Have you done any games or anything?' Will said to Mum.

Mum shook her head sadly.

Lucy said, 'Do you know what? This fête is very good, but it's terrible at the same time.'

In the café, Mum didn't say much, and Lucy asked if she was all right and she still didn't say much.

'Mum's ill,' Lucy said to Will when they were queueing for drinks.

Will was examining the things in his pockets. 'Is she?'

'Yes, she needs a cup of tea.'

The three Quigleys sat in the café, and Mum had a cup of tea, and Lucy had a cup of very milky tea, and Will had an orange squash, a piece of gingerbread, a rock cake, a cheese straw, four angel cakes and a packet of bubble gum.

'I'm sad you don't feel well, Mum,' Lucy

said. 'And we've stopped you doing everything all day, because we had to.'

'Yes, I know,' Mum said. She looked a bit shifty. 'But I do feel rather faint,' she added. 'Do you think you could get me another cup of tea?'

Lucy and Will went up together to the counter.

'Will,' Lucy said. 'She looks a bit grey.'

'Not as grey as Dad,' Will said. 'He's been on the rowing machine sixteen times. Is there enough money to get some more angel cakes?'

They got the cakes and a cup of tea for Mum, and went back to the table, and when they got there, Mum had gone.

'Did she say she was going, or did she just go?' Will said.

They stood there, looking around.

'Perhaps she's gone to vomit,' Will said. 'I hate vomiting in front of other people.'

Lucy was anxious. 'We have to find her, Will. Dad said we had to look after her, and now she's gone.'

'You're right,' Will said.

They went together out of the hall, and neither of them noticed that they were holding hands, but before they got outside there was an announcement over the tannoy: 'The skipping competition is about to begin.'

'That's you,' Will said. 'You'd better go.'

'I'm not going,' Lucy said. 'I haven't got anyone to do it with.'

Will looked sad and also worried. 'Don't look at me,' he said.

'I wouldn't skip with *you*,' Lucy said. 'Anyway, we have to find Mum.'

They went on towards the door, but before they reached it there was another announcement: 'Would Lucy Quigley please go to the central games area of the field? Lucy Quigley to the central games area.'

When Lucy got to the central games area, she found Mum waiting for her in a crowd of excited girls. Miss Petz and Mr Sheringham were waiting with a long rope and Miss Strickland was standing next to a table, and on the table was a large gold trophy.

'What are you doing, Mum?' Lucy said.

'I'm waiting for you.'

'Why?'

'Because we're the first pair to skip.'

Lucy thought about this. 'But you're not allowed, Mum. No games.'

'To hell with that,' Mum said.

'Oh, I see.' Lucy thought about this too. 'Won't Dad be cross with me for letting you skip?'

'Dad's too grey to be cross.'

The competition began. The first rhyme was *Two Six Nine*, and Mum and Lucy did it perfectly.

'Do you feel all right?' Lucy said afterwards. 'Aren't you feeling ill?'

Mum shook her head. She kicked her heels once or twice.

The pairs who hadn't done *Two Six Nine* without a mistake had to drop out. There were six pairs left. For the next round the rhyme was *Rosemary Apple Lemonade Tart*.

'Do you know this, Mum?' Lucy asked.

Mum grinned. She didn't often grin, but when she did she did it very well.

*Rosemary apple lemonade tart*
*Tell me the name of your true sweetheart*
*A, B, C, D, E, F, G, H, I, J, K, L, M*

Lucy couldn't think of a boy whose name began with M, so she shouted 'Mr Nelson', which is the name of Pippi Longstocking's monkey, and everyone laughed.

'Well done,' Mum said.

Now there were four pairs left in the competition. The rhyme for the next round was *Cinderella Dressed in Yella*.

'Oh, I like this one,' Lucy said.

*Cinderella dressed in yella*
*Went upstairs to kiss a fella*
*By mistake she kissed a snake*
*How many kisses did she take?*

Afterwards, Mum looked hot.

'If you want to stop now, it's all right,'

Lucy said. 'If you're not feeling well.'

'Hah!' Mum said. She didn't explain what she meant, but Lucy didn't think she wanted to stop.

Now there were only three pairs left. The

next rhyme was *Spanish Lady Turn Around*.
It was a long one.

'I don't know if I can do this,' Lucy said.

'Of course you can,' Mum said. 'We can
do it together. Look, Dad and Will are
watching us.'

Dad and Will were standing outside the
central games area, gazing at them. Dad
looked very grey, but he managed to give a
small cheer.

The rope began to twirl, and Mum
leaped into it.

*Not last night but the night before*
*Twenty-four robbers came knocking at my*
*door*
*As I went out to let them in*
*This is what they said to me*
*Spanish lady touch the ground*
*Spanish lady turn around*
*Spanish lady show off your shoes*
*Spanish lady that will do.*

After *Spanish Lady Turn Around* there were only two pairs left – Mum and Lucy, and two big girls. The judges were talking to each other. After a while, Miss Strickland spoke into the tannoy.

'Ladies and gentlemen, boys and girls,' she said. 'We are coming to the end of the skipping competition. By now we thought we would have a winner. But there are two pairs left. These two pairs,' she said, 'haven't made a mistake yet. It's very annoying. So the judges have decided that there will be one more round, and that this round will be extremely difficult.'

Then the judges whispered a bit more, and Miss Strickland announced the last song. *All in Together Girls*.

Lucy's face crumpled and she very nearly began to cry. 'But I've never heard of it,' she said. 'It must be a very new one, and I don't know how to do it.'

'No, it's not a new one,' Mum said excitedly. 'It's a very old one. And I know it! Listen, quickly now, and I'll tell you how to do it. All you have to remember is the months of the year.'

And when the time came, Mum and Lucy threw themselves forward into the turning rope, and Will gave a loud cheer, and Dad gave a feeble cheer, and everyone who was watching yelled and clapped, and they began.

*All in together girls*
*This fine weather girls*
*When you hear your birthday please jump out*
*January, February, March, April, May*

After the fête the Quigleys walked home together. They had quite a lot of stuff with them. Will was carrying a pile of second-hand *Beanos*. Mum was carrying a tray of seedlings she'd bought from the plant stall. And Lucy was carrying a large gold trophy. The trophy had fancy writing round the side of it saying *Parkside Skipping Champions*. Dad didn't carry anything.

Dad could hardly walk.

'It kept shifting,' he muttered from time to time.

When they got home, Dad lay down on the sofa in the back room, and Will lay on top of him and read *Beanos*, one after another. Mum offered to make pancakes for tea.

'Not burned ones,' she said.

'Will they look like knickers?' Will asked.

Mum shook her head.

Will grinned and slid off Dad. He started to empty his pockets. A battered pewter mug fell out, and a shirt embroidered with a scene of a bull fight.

'And while we eat them,' he said, 'I can show you a few of the bargains I picked up at the fête.'

# Friends with Lucy

# Friends with Lucy

The Quigleys decided to go on holiday to France in the summer. They talked about it before they went. Croissants came from France, and poodles, and wine, and a big bicycle race, Dad told them. People spoke a different language there, called French.

'French food is very good,' Mum said.

'So's French football,' Dad said. He wondered out loud if their tent would have a television.

They went to a campsite in a part of France called the Loire, and their tent was red and orange with real beds in it and, outside, a barbecue just for them. There wasn't a television, but there were lots of things to do – go-karts and bicycles to hire, ping-pong tables, a crazy golf course, an outdoor disco and a green lake where you could go out in a boat and watch the fish jump.

Will and Lucy were very excited. Will said the best thing about the camp was the swimming pool. It had slides and chutes and flumes and deep frothy pools. Best of all, it had fake battlements to fall off. Will's favourite thing was to climb the battlements, and be suddenly hit in the chest with a load of arrows, and fall, with a gurgly screamy death-cry, into the water. He got very good at it, and became so excited he could hardly control himself, and Mum and Dad were always having to tell him to calm down.

Lucy said the best thing on the campsite was the play area, a large sandy place full of climbing frames and roundabouts and swings and playhouses, and lots of children went there every day to play and chat and make friends. She decided to go to the play area every day too.

'Where are you going?' Mum and Dad would say, and she would say, 'Just to the play area.'

They would say, 'What are you going to do in the play area?' and she would say, 'I'm going to do some cartwheels. And then I'm going to do some handstands. And then I'm going to chat to someone and make a friend.'

Lucy was extremely interested in cartwheels and handstands, and she thought that the play area was the best place to practise them, because of being so sandy soft. But most of all she was interested in chatting and making friends.

One morning she went there, and did fourteen handstands in a row in a soft spot over by the smallest of the three playhouses. It was early, and the only other person

there was a girl in a blue frock sitting on a swing, watching her. Sometimes Lucy saw her the right way up, and sometimes upside down. She didn't mind the little girl watching her. Once the little girl smiled at her.

'Do you want to do handstands with me?' Lucy asked. The girl in the blue frock didn't say anything.

'Do you?' Lucy said. 'You can.'

The girl still didn't say anything. Then Lucy remembered what Mum and Dad had said about people from France not speaking English.

She sighed. 'It's not fair, is it?' she said. 'Because I can't ask you to do handstands with me because I don't know how to say it in French.' When the girl still didn't say anything, Lucy realized that she couldn't chat to her either, not even to tell her how unfair it was that she didn't know how to tell her she wanted to do handstands. And her heart really sank.

The girl stopped swinging and said
something to Lucy. It took Lucy by surprise.
It sounded like tongue-twisters and singing
and talking to babies all at once, and Lucy
couldn't understand her. Suddenly she felt
very shy.

'I'm sorry, I have to go now,' she said,
and she left the play area, and went back to
her tent.

Mum was playing badminton with a lady
from the tent next door. 'Did you make a
friend?' Mum said as Lucy went past.

Lucy didn't say anything. She went and
lay down on her bed, and was sad.

The next day, Lucy didn't go to the play area; she went to the pool with Will instead. She thought she might make a friend there. There were certainly lots of children at the pool. Lots in the shallow pools with the fountains, and lots in the deep pool, where people plunged in from the battlements, and lots going down the slides. Lucy liked the slides best. They were curvy and wavy, and she went down sitting or lying on her tummy or lying backwards *flap-splash* into the water. She went down the slides over and over. But she didn't

make a friend.

She lay on the towels with Mum and Dad, watching Will jump off the battlements. The battlements were too high for Lucy, even the lowest ones. Will could jump off them all except the highest one. He jumped in different ways. He fell with a gurgly screamy death-cry. He corkscrewed like a spinner dolphin. He

flipped forwards. He dived backwards. He sat in the air with a grin and a whoosh and squashed the water sideways. But he didn't quite dare to go off the highest battlement. In fact there was only one boy who jumped off the highest battlement. He was a tall boy with a round face, pink from the sun, and he always jumped the same way, holding his arms tight against his sides and hurtling down into the water. Sometimes he shouted, 'Gangway!' Whenever he jumped everyone watched him.

'Have you made a friend yet, Will?' Lucy said, when he came to lie down on the towels.

He grunted and put his nose into *The Beano*.

'Don't you want to make a friend, Will?' He shrugged.

'Don't you want to make friends with that jumping boy there?' she said.

He took his nose out of *The Beano*, and watched the boy with the round, pink face jump into the pool.

'That's the highest battlement he's jumping off,' he said in a wistful voice.

'You could be his friend if you wanted to,' Lucy said.

Will looked doubtful.

'You could. You could go and say hello to him, and have a chat, and he could tell you how to jump off the highest battlement. Would you like that, Will?'

Will didn't say anything, but he looked shy. His shy look was a sort of scowl.

'He speaks English,' Lucy said. 'I heard him.' She knew this was very important, because of the chatting, and she was pleased with herself for finding it out.

Will looked doubtful. 'I dunno,' he said.

'You don't have to be shy, Will,' Lucy said.

'I'm not shy,' Will said shyly, scowling.

A little later the same afternoon, when Lucy was waiting in the queue for the slides, she found herself standing next to the boy.

'Excuse me,' she said, very politely. 'Will you tell me how you jump off the highest battlement?'

The boy looked at her. 'I don't think you could do it,' he said at last. 'You have to be bigger, really.'

'It's not for me,' Lucy said. 'It's for my brother.'

'Who's your brother?'

Lucy pointed.

'The boy who can dive backwards?' he said.

Lucy thought about this. 'Can you dive backwards?' she asked.

The boy shook his head wistfully. 'Hardly anyone can dive backwards.'

Lucy thought a bit more. 'My brother could tell you how to dive backwards,' she said. 'If you come with me I'll ask him for you. He's quite nice,' she said. 'At least he is sometimes. Sometimes he does this thing with his face so it looks like he's about to get loud, but he hardly ever does, so you don't need to worry.'

After that, Will and the boy were always together. Sometimes they were leaping off the highest battlement, sometimes they were diving backwards.

'I'm glad Will's found a friend,' Dad said. 'Aren't you, Poodle?'

Lucy nodded. She didn't say anything, but she looked eager and sad at the same time.

The next day Lucy went back to the play area, but there was no one there she wanted to talk to, except the French girl in the blue frock. The girl was on the swing again, and they looked across the sand at each other. But Lucy knew she couldn't chat to her, so she went back to the tent.

Mum was there with a lady from the tent opposite. They were looking at a menu together.

'I was saying to Gertrude that we ought to try the restaurant here,' Mum said. 'We thought we all might try it together tonight.'

Gertrude was a nice lady with blonde hair and a baby with one wet tooth, and she smiled at Lucy.

'Did you find anyone to play with?' Mum asked.

Lucy shook her head, and went into the tent. Will was in the kitchen area testing his strength.

'I can lift you up, Dad. Dad, stand still while I lift you up.'

'Careful, Will.'

'I'm lifting you, Dad.'

'Will, stop it!'

'You're off ground, Dad.'

'Will, look out!'

There was a crash. After Will and Dad had argued for a bit, Dad went to the camp shop and Lucy went with him.

They walked up the lane holding hands. Dad was limping.

'Dad?' she asked. 'Can you talk French?'

'Not much, Poodle. I know a few important words, like please and thank you and cheers.'

'Do you know "Would you like to do cartwheels or Arab springs with me?"'

'I think I'd need help with that one.'

They walked between the trees and tents.

'Why don't you want to talk French, Dad? If you talked French you could make friends with French people.'

'I ought to learn, I know. But when French people talk to me, somehow I get confused and shy, and I can't think of anything to say. I know it's silly.'

In the shop they bought some bread, a bottle of washing-up liquid, a box of matches and some bottles of beer. Lucy liked the shop. It felt like outdoors: warm sunlight

came through the open door, and there was
sand on the floor where people had been
walking, and a smell of sun cream.

Dad was paying at the till, and Lucy was
waiting outside. As she watched, something
odd happened to Dad. A man in the queue
said something to him, and Dad went
funny. He put on his look of surprise, the
one where he looked as if someone had just
blown hard up his nose, and said something
back, and the other man started laughing.
Dad laughed too, though it wasn't Dad's
usual laugh, it was louder and longer and a

bit more mad. Then the man patted Dad on the arm, and Dad patted him back, though Lucy noticed that he was doing his surprised look again, and when Dad came out of the shop he was very distracted. He took Lucy's hand, and quickly walked away without looking back.

'Who's that man?' Lucy asked, trying to turn round as Dad pulled her along.

'Keep moving,' Dad said out of the corner of his mouth.

'He looks friendly. Why are we running away from him? Why did you do that look, as if someone's just blown up your nose?'

They walked one hundred yards at top speed, and then stopped to rest.

'A terrible thing just happened,' Dad said. 'Do you remember what I said about getting confused?'

'Yes.'

'Well, the lady at the cash till said something to me in French, and I got confused.'

'So you couldn't think of anything to say?'

'No, this time I said something straightaway.'

'But that was very good, Dad.'

'Only it wasn't French. It was German.'

Lucy thought about this. 'You said something in German to the French lady at the cash till?'

'Because of being confused,' Dad added.

'It doesn't seem *so* terrible,' Lucy said after a moment. 'I think it's more stupid than terrible.'

'That's not the terrible part,' Dad said. 'The terrible part is what happened next. A man in the queue began speaking German to me.'

'I didn't know you could speak German, Dad.'

'I can't. I know four words of German. I'd just used one, with the French lady, so I only had three left. But the man was so friendly, I didn't want to disappoint him. So I used one of my other words. Just to be friendly, in a German sort of way.'

'What did the word mean?'

'I'm not sure. It seemed to go down quite well. But now,' Dad groaned, 'he's bound to think I speak German. He might even think I *am* German. It's all to do with being confused,' he added. 'I don't think I could explain any of this. I just hope I don't see him again.'

After that, they saw the German man everywhere. He walked past the crazy golf course while they were playing, and Dad pretended to tie his shoelace until he'd gone.

Lucy said, 'But I think he looks friendly, Dad.'

Will said, 'Duh. How long does it take to tie your shoelace, Dad?' Will didn't realize what was going on.

They saw the German man at the lake, where Dad suddenly needed to go behind a tree, and they saw him again at the shop, where Dad began to search for something out of reach under the vegetable racks, and they saw him when they were playing Ping-Pong, and Dad bowed his head and examined the ball for several minutes, saying, 'I think it's cracked. Or is it a hair?'

And all the time Dad looked very distracted.

A few days later, Lucy went to the play area again, looking for someone to make friends with. There were two small boys fighting over what looked like a lollipop stick, but she didn't want to play with them. Besides, the stick was broken. There was a crowd of girls rushing round making each other wet with bottles of water, and she didn't want to play with them either. But there was a girl on her own playing 'two ball' against the side of one of the play houses. 'Two ball' was one of Lucy's favourite games, so she ran over to say hello, and when the girl turned round it was the girl she'd met before, the French girl in the blue frock.

'Oh!' Lucy said, and as soon as she said it she realised that 'oh' was wrong because it was English. She ought to say 'Oh!' in French instead. She didn't know what that

was, so she said, 'Woo!' but that didn't sound right, and the French girl looked a bit surprised.

Lucy took a deep breath, and smiled bravely, and said, 'Juicy whoosh two ball, rooby doo?' in the hope that it meant something like 'I like playing 'two ball', do you?' But the French girl just looked shocked.

Suddenly Lucy felt very shy, and said, 'I'm sorry, I have to go now,' and ran back to the tent.

Mum had gone swimming in the lake with a lady called Marcenda from the tent at the end of their row. Dad was sitting in a chair, partly reading a book and partly falling asleep. Lucy sat down next to him.

'Dad,' she said. 'If you started straight away, how long would it take you to learn German?'

'Too long,' Dad said.

'Too long for you to speak to the friendly German man?'

Dad nodded. 'It's a shame. He does look friendly, doesn't he? He's got a television in his tent. I saw it. He was watching a football game on it, but I was too far away to see who was playing. I mean, I couldn't risk getting too close.'

'Would it take me too long to learn French?' Lucy asked after a while. 'If I wanted to talk to someone on the camp.'

'I'm afraid so, Poodle.'

Lucy went into the tent and lay down on her bed and was sad again because she still didn't know how she was going to make a friend.

The next day she was practising her cartwheels in the lane when the German man walked past. He said hello and smiled at her, and she stopped doing cartwheels and smiled back. For a while she watched him walk up the lane. Something about him puzzled her, though at first she couldn't think what it was. She watched him walking up the lane, puzzling over it, then suddenly she understood. She started to walk after him.

The man went into the shop, and when he came out again he found Lucy waiting for him.

She had been practising what to say in her head so she wouldn't get it wrong.

'Excuse me,' she said very politely. 'You said hello to me.'

The man smiled. 'I did,' he said.

'You speak the English language,' she said, after a moment, to make sure.

The man smiled again, and nodded.

'So does my dad,' Lucy said. 'I mean, he's English. He isn't German,' she said.

'I know,' the man said.

'He does know four words of German,' Lucy said.

'I have heard two of them,' the man said.

Lucy had a good idea. 'Would you like to come back to our tent and talk to him?'

she asked. 'Now that you speak English and he isn't German.'

Lucy and the man were holding hands when they got to the Quigleys' tent. Dad was sitting in a chair outside, partly falling asleep and partly drinking a beer, and when he saw Lucy leading the German man towards him, his face went funny. He got to his feet in a rush, and made a little bow.

'It's all right, Dad,' Lucy said. 'You don't have to use the other two words. Gerd speaks English.'

And Gerd said, 'Your daughter has brought me to see you. Your daughter is a very

friendly girl.' And Lucy felt herself go pink.

After Dad had given Gerd a bottle of beer, Gerd asked if Dad would like to watch the football game on his television that evening, and Dad went pink.

Later that afternoon, when Mum came back from her swim, Lucy was sitting on her sleeping bag in the tent and Dad was trying to cheer her up.

'What is it, Lucy?' Mum said. 'What's the matter?'

'Nothing.'

'There is, Poodle,' Dad said.

'Isn't.'

Mum sat down next to her. 'Is it about friends?' she asked.

'No!' Lucy shouted. 'It's about no friends!'

They all talked about friends.

'Dad's got a friend,' Lucy said. 'And Will's got a friend. And you've got lots of friends. But I haven't got a friend at all.'

Mum and Dad said what a good and wonderful girl Lucy was to find friends for

Dad and Will, and they all lay together on Lucy's sleeping bag, talking about how friendly Lucy was, and how there were lots of people wanting to be friends with her, even though they hadn't found her yet. At last Lucy began to feel a bit better.

'And do you know what I think?' Dad said. 'I think you've played with Will very

nicely all holiday, I'm really proud of you. You've made a friend of your brother, and having a brother's nicer than having a friend.'

Both Lucy and Mum looked at him hard.

'Rubbish!' Lucy shouted, and she ran out of the tent.

Mum shook her head at Dad. 'You really played that wrong,' she said.

After she ran out of the tent, Lucy went to the play area and sat on the edge of the roundabout and kicked sand. After a while she practised a few handstands. The two boys who had fought over the broken lollipop stick were there, but Lucy didn't want to speak to them. She did a few cartwheels, and a few more handstands, and when she stopped the French girl was sitting on the swing watching her. She smiled at Lucy, and the smile was so friendly that at once Lucy felt pleased. She reached her hands up into the air for a second, then tipped herself suddenly upside down into the best handstand she'd ever done; it seemed to last for ages, and she could see the hot

blue sky above her.

When she came the right way up, the French girl was clapping her hands, and Lucy was so excited she jumped straight-away into a cartwheel and got her timing wrong and fell onto the ground.

The French girl got off the swing and ran over, and bent down to look at Lucy. She kissed her fingertips and touched Lucy gently on the knee. Then she straightened up, made a little bound, and flung herself into three cartwheels, one after the other.

Lucy clapped. She did a cartwheel, and another, and the French girl clapped.

Lucy smiled at her. 'Let's go on the climbing frame now,' she said. 'I want to show you something.' The girl stood there staring at her, and Lucy remembered.

'Oh,' she said. 'I forgot again. I can't talk to you.' She stood staring at the French girl and the French girl stood staring back.

Lucy thought for a moment.

'Well,' she said. 'I suppose it doesn't stop us going on the climbing frame.'

When they reached the climbing frame, the French girl jumped up, caught hold of one of the bars, and swung herself from one bar to another across to the other side.

'Wow,' Lucy said. 'I can't do that.' She shook her head. But the French girl nodded. She took Lucy's hands and showed her how to grip the bars, and showed her how to swing, first one hand, then the other, then the first one again. Lucy tried it, and got to the fourth bar before she fell off, which was better than she'd ever done before, and the French girl gave her a hug. After that, Lucy showed the French girl how to hang upside down from the highest bar, which wasn't at all frightening or dangerous if you did it the right way, and after a while the French girl let go with her hands, and hung there upside down, squealing a bit.

They played so happily, and for such a long time, that afterwards Lucy couldn't remember when they'd started to speak to each other. But they really must have, because Lucy knew that the French girl was

called Madeleine, just like Mum's friend, and Madeleine knew that Lucy was Lucy, because that was what she called her. And Lucy knew where Madeleine's tent was, and Madeleine knew that Lucy was the same age as her because she showed her on her fingers. Lucy supposed they had just started telling each other things without thinking, and pointing, and counting on their fingers, and it was funny how well you could talk with smiling and fingers. When they were tired of playing in the play area, they went to Madeleine's tent, and Lucy met her mother and father and her dog, which was very bushy and had bad breath.

Afterwards, Lucy took Madeleine to her own tent, to meet Mum and Dad, who were just beginning to get worried.

'This is Madeleine,' Lucy said. 'She's the same age as me, and her tent is near the dusty bit where you drive in at first, and she has a dog made of thick black wool, and a sister called Annette, and her mum gave me a drink you can't get in our country, and when Madeleine grows up she's going to be a gymnast. Oh, and she's my friend.'

Dad stepped forward. 'Very pleased to meet you, Madeleine,' he said. 'Is this the first time you've been on holiday in France?'

Madeleine stared at him. Dad stared at Lucy. Lucy stared at Dad.

Lucy said, 'Dad! Madeleine's French.'

'Oh,' Dad said. 'But then how . . .?'
But Lucy and Madeleine had already
gone into the tent, chatting.

# The End

**Dad**

**Mum**

**Mum**

**Lucy**

**Will**

**Dad**

**Mum**

**Mum**

**Lucy**

**Will**